# Gabriel

## and

# The Remarkable Pebbles

A FABLE

*by Carol Hovin*

Sunstar
PUBLISHING LTD.

GABRIEL and the Remarkable Pebbles
by Carol Hovin
© United States Copyright, 1996
Sunstar Publishing, Ltd.
116 North Court Street
Fairfield, Iowa 52556

Cover Design:  Roland Dempsey

Library of Congress Catalog Card Number: 96-069495
ISBN: 1-88742-06-1

Readers interested in obtaining further information on the subject
matter of this book are invited to correspond with
The Secretary, Sunstar Publishing, Ltd.
116 North Court Street, Fairfield, Iowa 52556

To

the dreamer within.


May the loveliest

creations

come forth into Light.

# Acknowledgements

The author expresses immeasurable gratitude for the support and technical assistance readily and skillfully given by Arne Hovin. Special thanks to Michelle Orton for valuable professional help and to world enthusiasts, Mike and Randi Ann Rigg for inspiration and assistance. The author is most grateful to Zannah and to Linda Vephula, publisher *Angel Times* magazine (vol 1, issue 3, 1995) for permission to use the narration by Zannah. Lastly, great appreciation is extended to master airbrush artist Roland Dempsey for the intricate and inspired cover design and to Rodney Charles and Elizabeth Pasco of Sunstar Publishing Ltd. for their perceptive editorial guidance.

# Contents

# Beginnings in an Orphanage

"Never, never in all of France could there be such a difficult child as you, Gabriel," declared the Headmistress as she forcefully hit her desk top with a clinched hand. "In all my years at this orphanage, you are the most impossible nine-year-old I have ever encountered!"

Not only was Headmistress Mademoiselle Martinez often upset with Gabriel's astounding behavior, but so was every member of her staff. They engaged in much shaking of heads, rolling of eyes and shrugging of shoulders over the peculiar ways of this gentle-hearted boy. Far from being a naughty child, he was rather just very unusual. Sometimes revealing words would come clearly to Gabriel's mind, sometimes pictures of explanation would appear before his closed eyes, and with open eyes sometimes he'd see what others couldn't. And he had the audacity to tell of these things!

Gabriel sat patiently before the Headmistress for yet another scolding in a seemingly endless succession of scoldings. Curiously, he appeared neither upset nor fearful. His slender body was relaxed, his dark eyes gazed serenely into Mademoiselle Martinez's stormy face. To her consternation, he appeared undisturbed by the severe rebuke she was dispensing.

At the very peak of this reprimand, Gabriel felt compelled to lower his head and close his eyes. Instantly, his mind produced a picture of Mademoiselle when she was a child. Mademoiselle's father was standing before her shouting angrily, "Don't ever speak again about the elves and fairies you claim to see in the garden, nor about the birds and the trees that talk to you!"

Gabriel observed that the light of Mademoiselle's childhood was nearly blown out by the fury of her father's words. Only a delicate flicker remained, surrounded by darkness. The fear and resentment from this early life event lay hidden inside the now grown-up Mademoiselle Martinez, and appeared to Gabriel like a dark cloud. Yet, he knew that her innocent heart was longing to open once again as it had been so long ago. Furthermore, he now understood that she had purposely chosen to work with orphans, for in the giving of comfort and small delight to them, she had hoped to recover the joy lost as a young child.

But today, Mademoiselle was in such a state of agitation

over Gabriel's recent conduct that it allowed the remembrance of her old fear and resentment to spill upon Gabriel once again. She was unaware, however, of the real reason for her intense anger.

Mademoiselle scowled at the boy who sat before her with his head bowed, eyes closed, seemingly unaffected by her sharp words. "Oh, what an exasperating child you are," she reinforced. "You can't have conversations with animals, you can't see elves or fairies or angels, you can't know what's going to happen before it happens," she shouted! "If you keep insisting that you can, no one will ever want to adopt you. You must not reveal anything of this sort of nonsense to the people who come here to look you over and get acquainted," she declared. "Otherwise, you and I will be forced to live together for years and years in this orphanage, and I think I should grow quite mad from the constant aggravation."

Gabriel opened his eyes and, in a gentle manner, told Mademoiselle, "You need not worry about my being a permanent burden to you." And he added, "I will soon be adopted by a loving, caring couple. I just know the time has come for this to happen." But alas, instead of being happy with him over this possibility, Mademoiselle Martinez was infuriated again by the thought that Gabriel could presume to know more about adoption proceedings than she did. "It will certainly be a surprise to me," she replied sarcastically.

Scarcely a month before, Gabriel had been sitting in the very same chair in her office being scolded for telling little Babette that she would be adopted soon. Babette, in her excitement and naiveté, had babbled about her would-be parents to Mademoiselle who definitely had no such arrangements recorded in her appointment book. To Mademoiselle's dismay, however, the next day an admirable couple did indeed come unannounced and immediately fell in love with the dear little Babette. At once they began filing the necessary adoption papers, just as Gabriel had foretold.

Mademoiselle's mind shifted to another recent occurrence when the pet dog of the orphanage lay desperately ill. Gabriel had told Mademoiselle, "He has eaten some rotten meat while browsing in the alley behind the orphanage. The dog confessed to me of having been unable to resist the tempting discovery, even though his natural instincts warned him."

With tight lips and a deep frown, Mademoiselle had dismissed the entire conversation and then telephoned the local veterinarian. The doctor who came to examine the dog was slow in diagnosing the problem because of several possibilities. Reluctantly, Mademoiselle finally suggested, "Do you think the dog may have eaten spoiled meat he found in someone's garbage?"

"Yes, thank you," said the doctor, "that now confirms my suspicion of his symptoms. We shall give your dog this strong medicine immediately. And I'm sure he will recover and not be tempted again by the menu in the alley."

For Gabriel to be so confident regarding the dog's difficulty, and even presume to have had a conversation with the dog, only made Mademoiselle more frustrated and more determined to punish him. It was an endless exasperation for her that this young boy could be so sure of his disclosures, and then be proven so right.

Time and again, he knew things before they occurred and certainly much before she herself knew. He also knew of her secrets about those things at the orphanage which had not gone as well as Mademoiselle had expected. She had kept these hidden from her staff, but seemingly never from Gabriel. Without exchanging words, Mademoiselle Martinez knew he was well aware of her failings.

Her thoughts then returned to the moment. Although

she wished this provocative child might at last be adopted, Mademoiselle remained doubtful. Over the years when her expectations had been high for a favorable outcome, the potential parents would abruptly end their interaction with Gabriel and not offer her an explanation.

"Oh, Gabriel, are you and I destined to spend our lives together in conflict?" she queried with a sigh of resignation. "You must not let your peculiar ways be known if you ever hope to be adopted!"

This aspect was difficult for Gabriel to understand because he assumed others knew in the same manner as he did. But, Gabriel now comprehended how critical it was that his conversations not seem strange to prospective parents.

The telephone rang as Mademoiselle was concluding this latest and most severe scolding. "You are dismissed, Gabriel," she said sharply, and then directed her attention to the caller. This telephone interruption was a welcomed relief for the Headmistress.

# *Anticipation within an Outing*

*T*he local banker was calling Mademoiselle Martinez to confirm the details of the annual orphanage trip to le parc d'attractions sponsored by his bank. "Yes," she said, "all is in order, and I plan to announce the trip today at the noontime meal."

Mademoiselle had purposely chosen midday to inform the children of this forthcoming event, in hopes that upon hearing the news their boisterous enthusiasm might be diffused through the afternoon. Then by bedtime, perhaps the children would fall asleep more readily and be rested for the festivities awaiting next day.

In the morning, Gabriel awoke with an instant remembrance of the day's importance. He wanted to run straight away to the bus and be in the park at once. But instead, he took a full breath to slow himself down, for he had nearly forgotten to breathe as the rush of anticipation increased within him. Gabriel loved adventures and looked forward to this one with great expectations. He felt extremely happy and offered a silent but wholehearted "Thank You" to the banker for again inviting the children of the orphanage to a holiday in the park.

While swiftly pulling on his clothes, he recalled other outings to the park, other years. But he'd never before had such tingling he felt now in his body. It was as if sparkles of light danced in every cell and made it difficult for him to be calm. Nevertheless, he deliberately sat down on the edge of his bed to ponder this new, electrifying state of himself.

"Is it just that I'm so glad to be going on the trip once again, or is there something even more exciting to happen for me?" He breathed deeply to quiet himself and closed his eyes. What he saw in his mind was a picture of two people in the park walking toward him with outstretched arms to welcome him to their hearts.

"Oh, is this the day," shouted Gabriel aloud in the dormitory, "is this the day my parents will come for me?" Because the boys nearby were so busy dressing themselves in play clothes for the excursion, they were not the least aware of his outburst.

Shortly after breakfast, of which Gabriel ate so little, the hired bus arrived on schedule. The other children, all younger than he, laughed and chattered together as they boarded the bus to take their seats. The babies in their carriages were wheeled to a space at the rear. "What a bright sunny day," thought Gabriel, "even the dusty cobblestone streets glisten in the morning light and all the buildings seem newly painted." As the bus approached the park, it was just as he had remembered it, only now more green and sparkling.

Gabriel walked about the various enticing rides, choosing first one and then another, amidst the squeals and delights of the laughing children. All the while, he felt a new liveliness within that demanded attention. His heart was already beating faster as if aware of the joy to come. "I know there is no way I can force my adoption to happen, and maybe it won't happen today, or maybe not even this year." Yet, a feeling of anticipation remained inside him, and he couldn't help predicting, "My dream picture really will come true, and this is the day I'll be meeting my new parents!"

At noon, the children came eagerly to the picnic area when they were called. All details of this lunch had been thoughtfully prepared by the banker and his staff. The large wooden tables were clad in blue and white checkered cloths, and in the center of each was a colorful bouquet of orange marigolds, blue bachelor buttons and rosy cosmos pleasantly arranged in a white vase. The tables were set with utensils, white pottery plates, blue napkins, and blue glasses filled with mineral water.

Gabriel stood in awe at the sight before him, believing this was the most festive picnic ever! He slowly surveyed the contents of the tables laden with baskets of crusty rolls, long loaves and round loaves of fresh bread, platters of cheese, some soft, some firm, bowls of salad greens dressed in olive oil and lemon juice, a potato salad mixed with black olives and pieces of sweet red peppers. Fruit trays were brimming with bunches of green and purple grapes, with pears and nectarines too.

As he gazed at so abundant a display of food, Gabriel felt his appetite returning in full force, and he joined the others in eating with gusto. As a surprise for the conclusion of the feast, each was served a small fruit tart. His tart had a thin custard base layered with slender slices of peaches, five raspberries, half a blue-purple plum and topped with a strawberry. Then a light, sweet glaze had been drizzled over the fresh fruit pieces. Gabriel and the other children never tasted such a delectable dessert.

Following this lavish meal, the children began playing

games on the wide, green lawn of the park. Some tossed balls and others threw bean bags to each other. The younger ones joined hands with adults in circle games. Gabriel gathered some older children to play soccer, and soon a spirited game was in progress.

As he was about to deliver a swift kick to the ball, Gabriel stopped in mid-action. On the far side of the green, a man and woman were walking towards the children at play. As the couple continued in Gabriel's direction, he could scarcely breathe for fear they would walk right past him. But no, they smiled gently, each one, and then the man complimented him by saying, "You have a fine soccer style, young man."

With a smile, the woman stepped towards Gabriel and said, "My name is Nicole and this is my husband, Jean-Pierre Honoré."

Gabriel nodded to each and then replied, "And I am Gabriel." As he looked into their friendly faces, his heart leaped with such happiness that speech was impossible. These were the very same two people he'd seen in his inner picture that morning!

 # A Meeting of Hearts and Minds

*N*icole asked Gabriel, "Would you like to sit down here with us so we might talk together for awhile?" He agreed and after having instructed the children to continue their soccer game, he joined the Honorés in the shade of a tall plane tree by the edge of the field.

She began the conversation by telling him, "We read in our local paper about the orphanage picnic today, and we've come in deliberate search for the child of our longing."

Then Jean-Pierre added, "We stood nearly hidden under the dense foliage of some linden trees at the park's edge and watched all you children for quite some time. Always our eyes were drawn back to you, Gabriel."

When Gabriel heard these words, a great wave of joy swept through his entire body, but he held his feelings inside. He didn't want to spoil his opportunity by appearing overly eager, before this couple might be ready to parent him.

They asked Gabriel many questions, not in a quizzical manner, but rather from their eagerness to begin to know him. Gabriel willingly answered regarding his age, his years in the orphanage, his favorite studies and interests, the colors he preferred and the games he liked to play. And he told of his fondness for the other children and the dog of the orphanage. However, he carefully watched his words so that he wouldn't divulge his peculiar ways of knowing things. Nothing must ruin this new relationship.

Gabriel noticed how pretty Nicole was as he listened carefully to her telling him that they lived outside Paris on a wondrous old boat. "It's named FRIENDSHIP," she explained, "to honor our university days in England where we first met each other. We've made the boat seem spacious inside by adding many built-in pieces of furniture. I myself have taken much pleasure in decorating with plants and pictures, lamps and curtains and pillows to create a cosy feeling in our boat home."

Nicole's husband was a kind and soft-spoken man, but Gabriel could tell he was also very strong. "I ride the train into Paris for my job," Jean-Pierre said, "and Nicole does her work in a tiny office right on the boat.

We are both trained in geology, which is the study of earth's formation and its many rock types. On weekends and holidays, we sometimes enjoy flying about France in a small rented airplane that each of us can pilot." Gabriel's eyes grew wide with wonder and anticipation. The three of them sat together comfortably for awhile without saying anything. Then Nicole knelt on one knee before Gabriel to look directly into his dark brown eyes with her own softer, lighter ones. "I'm so very glad to talk with you today," she said, "and I know good things are about to happen because of our becoming acquainted." Jean-Pierre nodded in agreement.

"We had no thoughts before of contacting the orphanage because Jean-Pierre and I felt a baby or a very young child would not fit so easily into our lives. But, after reading about the outing in the park, something compelled us to come this day. We have no children of our own," Nicole revealed, "and we would welcome one so fine as you into our hearts. Our hearts have no beginning and no ending, and you would never be without our love."

Gabriel's own heart filled with such a strong longing to be with these wonderful and caring people. He knew they would understand him, and one day he could safely disclose more of his knowing self.

At that moment, Mademoiselle Martinez called all the children to board the bus for their return to the orphanage. As they stood up to leave, Jean-Pierre told Gabriel, "We'll see you again very soon, we promise you." Gabriel hugged these parting words tightly to himself so he wouldn't lose them and then climbed into the bus. He hurriedly took a window seat, and his eyes followed Nicole and Jean-Pierre leaving the park as they waved goodbye, "au revoir."

"Oh, they are the ones!" spoke his heart, and Gabriel felt tears of joy flow into his eyes. He swiftly wiped away any evidence, but his smile remained all during the return ride to the orphanage. "This has been my most glorious day!" he proclaimed to himself. "Any fears I might have had about ever being adopted are completely gone. Nicole and Jean-Pierre are the ones I've been waiting for all my nine years!"

# New Home, New Parents

Less than a week later, Gabriel was called into Mademoiselle Martinez's office. He was unsure of what the expected scolding would be about this time. He couldn't think of anything he'd said or done these past few days that would have provoked Mademoiselle. As he entered her office, for once she was not frowning at him. "I have wonderful news for you," she said.

And then Gabriel saw them! There stood Nicole and Jean-Pierre, each smiling so genuinely and lovingly upon him. Yes, it was true! Mademoiselle said all the necessary adoption papers had been completed, and he was free to leave the orphanage just as soon as he'd packed his belongings.

Nicole had brought a small duffel bag, and Gabriel stowed it quickly with a pair of sturdy shoes, a sweater, two pairs of shorts, a pair of long pants, several shirts, underwear, socks, a wool hat, gloves and a light jacket. There was room to add the books he'd received each Christmas and the occasional toy which had come his way over the years. He took extra care in packing a small wooden sailboat he especially treasured and then put on his beloved baseball cap before leaving the dormitory.

Gabriel said goodbye to his pal, the dog, and to the children, telling them, "I'll come visit you when I can." Solemnly he shook hands with the cook and thanked her for all the meals he'd been served and for the little treats she'd prepared as a secret surprise for him.

"I wish you great happiness, Gabriel," she said and gave him a tender farewell hug.

Next, Gabriel thanked the housekeeper for all the laundry and mending and cleaning she'd done as her part in caring for him these nine years. He thanked the teacher for helping him accelerate in mathematics and learn many things of the world beyond the orphanage walls. Lastly, he shook hands with Mademoiselle Martinez as he thanked her for allowing him to remain so long under the care of the orphanage. And then he was out the door of l'orphelinat du Paris, walking hand in hand with his new parents!

Parked at the curb was a small, dark blue Renault, and Gabriel nimbly settled into the back seat beside his duffel bag. With Jean-Pierre at the wheel, they swirled easily through the heavy traffic of the city and headed south to their boat home. Gabriel felt so completely at ease with Nicole and Jean-Pierre that conversation seemed unnecessary. Apparently they felt the same, for the only exchange among the three was smiles of contentment as they each savored this moment in time.

Gabriel looked intently out the windows to see all he could of Paris. As they drove further south, he noticed the bustle of city traffic had gradually subsided. Soon Jean-Pierre turned the car toward the river Seine, and Gabriel knew they were approaching the boat. Around the next bend the car came to a stop by a dockside where his new home was tied up. "What a great old boat!" exclaimed Gabriel. It was painted white, with a trim of deep blue-green that matched the color of the ocean in his geography book. FRIENDSHIP was handsomely engraved on a brass plate affixed to her bow. "She's so beautiful, just beautiful!"

Catching hold of his duffel, Gabriel was out of the car in no time and up the gangplank, followed by his new parents. Jean-Pierre unlocked the door to the living quarters and Gabriel stepped inside. He immediately felt embraced in the loving warmth of Nicole's wonder-working. Everything was so neatly arranged and everything offered an invitation to beauty and comfort. "I feel at home at last!" he said with pure joy in his voice. "To think that I, Gabriel of l'orphelinat, would be living on this magical boat and be loved by two such wonderful people!"

"Come now, Gabriel, and see your own quarters," Nicole suggested. "We've prepared this little port side cabin just for you. You'll be able to view the many boats and barges on the river and even see the stars at night."

After stepping into the room, his eyes opened wide with surprise at what lay before him. A wooden bed had been cleverly built into the outside wall so the porthole would be near his head. On the bed was a blue-green comforter to keep out the night chill of the river and underneath was a large drawer for storage. A woven wool rug in multi-colors graced the wooden floor with its warmth. There would be plenty of room for his clothes in a floor to ceiling built-in closet at the aft end of the cabin. And in the corner of the opposite end near the door, Gabriel saw his new desk with bookshelves above, a nautical desk lamp and a captain's chair. Artful pictures chosen specially for him hung on the walls. "Oh, am I ever a young prince of the sea!" he exclaimed enthusiastically.

Then, Gabriel searched in his duffel to find the wooden toy boat. This he placed on a shelf above his desk and hung his beloved baseball cap on a peg nearby. With eyes still aglow and open arms, he turned to tightly hug first Nicole and then Jean-Pierre. The hugs were returned in kind, and Gabriel could feel the happiness that swirled from heart to heart in beautiful circles.

# A Dream of Pebbles

*T*he days flowed swiftly for Gabriel. Nicole taught his school lessons in the morning, and in the afternoon she worked in her tiny office. Gabriel was free to play whenever he had completed his assignments and often went up on deck to watch the activity on the river. Both working barges and pleasure boats passed by frequently, and he always gave a wave of greeting to the people on board. He took delight in their friendly waves in return. He could even see the trains on the opposite bank of the river, as they traveled to and from Paris with their many passengers.

Some days he walked the dockside to visit with boat neighbors. At least once a week, he did his chore of polishing everything in the wheelhouse and on the upper deck. And in his imagination, he sailed on many a voyage while he cleaned and shined the fittings.

One afternoon, Gabriel sat in his cabin in deep thought for a very long time. Nicole passed by on several errands from her office to the galley, and finally she asked, "Is there something on your mind, Gabriel, that you might want to talk about?"

"I'm supposed to remember something from a dream I had last night, but I've forgotten it all. I think it has to do with rocks and the three of us, but that's all I can recall."

"Oh, Gabriel, if you don't try so hard, I think you will remember whatever it is that's so important for you," Nicole suggested. "Come into my office and look through the tall filing drawers. Perhaps one of the rocks in that collection will help you recall your dream, while you're having a good time looking at the great variety of rocks from many places on our planet."

He did indeed have a grand time. In fact, Gabriel spent more than a week of afternoons there, quietly holding each rock. The rocks spoke to him inwardly and gave him brief mental pictures behind his closed eyes that told of how they had formed and where they had lived. This new and exhilarating experience clearly indicated that there was yet more for him to know about rocks.

# Night Messenger

"Hush
be silent
breathe in peace
I bring to you a vision
the glory of a child's dream
a message for a mission
and on the parchment
torn and rolled
scroll cradled in my palm
unrolled before a dreamer's eyes
proclaiming heaven's calm
believe in me
believe in you
believe in all that's love
awaking with night's memory
confirmed by morning's dove"

Narration by Zannah

# Reappearance of the Dream

O ne night as Gabriel's head came to rest on the bed pillow and he had closed his eyes for sleep, an image appeared in his mind of a round and smooth, gray-colored pebble. It was like none he had seen in Nicole's collection. If he could have touched it, he was certain it would have felt soft as velvet. Within the depths of his heart, he had a strong feeling that the gray pebble held some very special meaning for him. He smiled to himself as the gentle rocking of the boat in the river lulled him into the deepest of sleep.

Sometime during the night, an angel friend appeared in his dreams and spoke, "Gabriel, you remembered! Good boy! That small stone and many, many more exactly like it will have great meaning, not only for you but for the billions of people on earth. These pebbles will help people be so much more comfortable and, at the same time, greatly help to conserve the planet's natural resources. You will not forget anymore. We are here to help you and Nicole and Jean-Pierre. You three are together at last. All is exactly right, all is in perfect position. We surround you in Love." She smiled upon

Gabriel as his dream ended and he continued to sleep.

In the morning, he did remember his dream just as he was awakening. He allowed it to come completely to mind so he wouldn't forget any details. Would he dare to tell Nicole and Jean-Pierre? Yes, he would risk it, because they were also a part of the dream and because he felt so very safe with these two extraordinary people.

The Honoré family was seated together at the little table in the compact galley that Sunday morning, helping themselves to a hearty breakfast. Nicole had placed on the table a pitcher of freshly squeezed orange juice, a large bowl of assorted fruit, and a very long loaf of bread called baguette still warm from the local baker's oven. Gabriel was blissfully spreading sweet butter and jam on his piece of the baguette.

There was no train to catch, no school lesson, no urgent chore. It was just a leisurely time of being with each other. The sun shone brightly through the portholes into the interior of the boat. Its warmth and cheeriness encouraged Gabriel to speak of his dream from the night before. He told them all details, exactly as he remembered. And when finished he asked, "You do believe in dreams and angels, don't you?" While waiting for their answer, he held his breath momentarily in spite of feeling sure of their affirmative response.

"Yes, indeed," replied Nicole with a smile, "I've had hunches in the daytime and dreams at night that have been very helpful to me, and I know that Jean-Pierre has too, but perhaps not as often as I. Right after breakfast, let us look through my rock samples. You, Gabriel, look for the stone that most resembles that of your dream," she suggested.

They all three searched the specimen drawers, and Gabriel identified one he said was similar in color, another similar in shape, and finally one that was similar in texture. "Now," said Gabriel, "if we could just put all these qualities into one small rock, I think it would be very much like the gray pebble of my dreams."

Nicole carefully studied the rock samples, noting the distinct characteristics of each. She had a hunch that the stone they were looking for would be found in only a few particular places in the world. She meticulously reviewed her geological maps, jotting down several possible locations.

Then she laid her pen aside and said, "Now let's rest our thoughts concerning the gray pebble. It's too beautiful a day outside not to be enjoying it. We'll pack a picnic lunch and go bicycling along the river's edge, and then over the rise to the farm fields beyond."

Nicole deftly filled a large wicker basket with three bottles of mineral water, an oblong loaf of peasant bread, some cheese, a spicy herb and bean spread, hot radishes, tender carrots and cherry tomatoes. Last to be tucked into the basket was Gabriel's favorite, a flaky crescent-shaped pastry known as croissant.

The outing was glorious and Gabriel enjoyed it all immensely. Upon their return shortly after sunset, they sat together at the little galley eating rye bread and generous servings of Nicole's creamy vegetable soup of potatoes, carrots and large leeks. Following this nourishing supper, Gabriel was quite content to slip into his cosy bed and soon was fast asleep.

# The Meaning
## of the Gray Pebbles

During the night's sleep, Gabriel's dreams brought forth an image of the soft, gray pebble again. This time he could look right into the heart of it and see brilliant sparks of light which didn't appear on its surface. His angel friend came into this dream and moved her hands and fingers over the pebble in an uncommon manner. Then she produced a pan of water and placed the pebble in it. Gabriel was amazed when he saw the water become hot enough to cook a meal.

Following this revelation, the angel told Gabriel, "Pay close attention to what you will see next." She blew softly on the glowing pebble to cool it and then put it on his blue-green quilt. With a different patterning of her hands and fingers than before, the pebble now became seven more pebbles identical to the original one. This multiplication occurred instantly and at a rate far faster than Gabriel's eyes could perceive.

"Place one of these pebbles on to your pillow, Gabriel, and repeat the hand and finger movements in exactly the pattern you just witnessed," requested the angel.

When Gabriel had completed the pattern as he remembered it, there on his pillow seven more pebbles appeared beside the first one. He smiled in great delight! Next, the angel told Gabriel, "Take these eight pebbles from your pillow and the seven remaining ones from the bed quilt and place them in this iron pot I give you." The angel then carefully instructed him how to impress on these fifteen gray pebbles the pattern that she first used to produce heat from the single pebble. Great warmth began to radiate from the pebble-filled pot after he had repeated her procedure.

"If one pebble is enough to boil water in a cooking pan, fifteen pebbles are enough to heat a small house," she explained. "You have just seen how the small, gray pebbles will provide instant, clean and very inexpensive heat for all people on earth to cook their food and to warm their dwellings." Gabriel was astonished by the magnitude of this possibility!

"There is one more important feature to tell you about before I must be on my way to participate in other dreams." The angel produced a glass filled with water and handed it to Gabriel, saying, "Smell the contents, and then take a tiny sip." Which he did. "Now, tell me your experience of smell and taste," she requested.

"It doesn't smell very good and I don't like the taste either," he commented.

After the angel had instructed him to place one pebble into the glass of water, she moved her hands and fingers in a new geometric pattern above the container. "Now Gabriel, smell the water first and then take a good, big sip," she said. He did just that and was amazed to find it smelled and tasted like the sparkling pure water he drank in the high mountains one weekend with Nicole and Jean-Pierre.

"Remember this dream, Gabriel," the angel declared, "for the pebbles are to warm the dwellings, cook the food, and purify the water for the people on your planet. The pebbles will also provide the energy of heat when the people wish to create the many things that bring them pleasure. The stones never lose their energy. All that is required is that they be placed in sunlight for one day of every year. This will remind them of their Source. Your engineers will do wonders with these pebbles, you'll see," she concluded.

"I go now, but you and Nicole and Jean-Pierre are always in our hearts. We are but a thought away from you at any moment."

When Gabriel awoke in the morning, he sat straight up in bed trying his best to understand why he was feeling so keenly happy. "It's like having Christmas and my special day and the day I was adopted, all at once!" he said aloud to himself. Whatever it was, he could only sit there and smile for the joy of it. "Ah, yes," he thought, "it was related to a dream again of the gray pebble." He held himself very still in both mind and body, and soon his dream returned in full remembrance.

Jean-Pierre had taken the train to Paris and Nicole was busy at her work by the time Gabriel had sorted out his dream and gotten into his clothes. He stood quietly at the door to Nicole's office, waiting for her to finish a letter she was writing. He was bursting to tell, but knew it best to wait till she had completed her task. At last he confided all his dream to her, and she was as thrilled as he.

"I've never seen nor heard of anything like what you just described about the small gray pebbles and their potential, Gabriel, but I don't say it's nonsense either," she commented. "We will just let what is to be, be. Share with us your dreams and mind pictures, and together we shall know what to do as it all unfolds," advised Nicole. "But for now, we'll attend to your school lessons just as soon as you've eaten breakfast."

# A Golden Daydream

The following week, Gabriel was seated in the bow of the FRIENDSHIP with the afternoon sun pouring upon him. He dreamily envisioned himself preparing to land on a strange, tropical island. As commander of his ship, he'd ordered the crew to row him ashore in the dingy. With nothing to do but enjoy the ride, the youthful Capitaine Gabriel Honoré closed his eyes in the warmth and gentleness of the day, while the steady sound of oars being pulled through the water reached his awareness.

In that place of reverie, further mind pictures could easily present themselves to him. And they did. A lady of golden light appeared and told Gabriel that he, Nicole, and Jean-Pierre would be traveling round the world, searching for locations of the special gray pebbles. "The three of you will be needing funds to pay for your expenses during this momentous adventure," she advised. Then she pointed to a valley that looked somewhat familiar to Gabriel. As he took a closer look, he detected a vein of gold running through a rock formation in the cliffs nearby. The angel lady smiled and assured him, "You will find this newly-surfaced gold, which only you three Honorés will be able to see."

"The place where you will locate the gold is on public land," she said. "You are to use these large gold nuggets to finance your search, development and distribution of the gray pebbles, which are to become a major source of heat and purification for the comfort and well-being of all people, everywhere," she proclaimed.

"Your design engineers will create heating and purifying devices which will be simple, efficient, and very, very affordable for all. Eventually, all great and small cities will use these stones in their municipal water works, and the people will again drink sparkling, pure water. They will once more cook and bath and water their gardens and fields with the cleanest of waters," said the angel of golden light.

Capitaine Gabriel thought to himself, "I must get back to my ship at once and sail home to France so I can tell Nicole and Jean-Pierre what this golden angel just revealed to me." No long return voyage was necessary, however. As Gabriel opened his eyes, he realized he was already home on the bow of the FRIENDSHIP. He only had to walk below deck to Nicole's office.

Her door was open and she was folding up books and putting away papers when Gabriel appeared. He told her of the daydream of gold and what they were to do with it. The two of them sat together for the remainder of the afternoon, determining where the gold vein might be. Since the site seemed rather familiar to Gabriel, he said, "I'm certain it will be in France where all three of us have recently been. It wasn't until you adopted me that I've done any traveling at all beyond the city of Paris."

They poured over topographic maps and soon located several possible sites. "It's just like a treasure hunt," said Gabriel, "it's so exciting!" Nicole nodded in hearty agreement, and they shared their enthusiasm with Jean-Pierre who had just stepped inside the boat on his return from Paris.

The weekend plans were immediately set, and Gabriel had but two days to wait. He diligently studied his school lessons, and even asked Nicole if he might look through some of her geology books. Gabriel and Nicole, in particular, spent many hours speculating on this latest development of the dream information.

 # The Search Begins

*A*nd now the golden day had arrived, the search would begin. Food enough for lunch and supper was placed into picnic baskets and, with hopeful hearts, the treasure hunters walked down the gangplank to their car. Nicole sat beside Jean-Pierre in the front seat with a map held in her hand. Gabriel sat quietly in the back, too excited for conversation. The widest of smiles decorated his charming face and was captured in the rearview mirror. Jean-Pierre couldn't help but smile broadly to himself at the sight of Gabriel's joyful expectation.

They drove some miles to the airport where they had reserved a small airplane to fly over areas Nicole thought had possibilities. After the car was parked under the shade of a generous elm tree, the three strode across the runway to their rental plane. Jean-Pierre flew the aircraft as low as permitted over several areas pinpointed on their map, but so far, none appeared to Gabriel as the one in his daydream. Nicole and Jean-Pierre were very patient with him, even though they hoped each pass over a new valley would be the one Gabriel would recognize. This kind of 'knowing' was new to them, and both felt it important that they should work together in a helpful manner while all three learned to become a unified search team.

Jean-Pierre had piloted the plane over eight valley sites without success, and now they were approaching the last one marked on Nicole's map. When this valley came into Gabriel's view, he immediately sat up at attention. His whole body responded to the message his eyes were giving him. "It's the valley of the golden daydream!" he exclaimed.

Since the location of this sighting was not too far from the airport, they returned the rental plane. And after lunch under the big elm tree, they drove their car back to the ninth spot on Nicole's map of possibilities. As they proceeded through the valley, Nicole and Gabriel said at the same moment, "Stop here!" Jean-Pierre quickly responded and brought the Renault to a halt by the roadside. It did look familiar to them, and they remembered having picnicked there only a few weeks ago, along side the rippling river with the towering cliffs beyond.

Gabriel and Nicole got out of the car and stood with eyes closed for a moment, each waiting for some sort of inspiration to come that would give a clue to the gold source. As Gabriel opened his eyes, a shaft of light bounced off the upper area of the cliffs beyond the river, directly within his line of sight. After explaining what he'd just seen, Gabriel suggested, "It's as if that light were a beacon clearly pinpointing the location of the gold vein for us."

They eagerly followed this lead and came upon a suitable place where some large boulders allowed them to cross the rapidly flowing river in safety. When they reached the opposite shore, Jean-Pierre chose a reliable route for them to scramble up the steep face of the cliffs to the upper area where Gabriel had seen the beam of light. They all gathered at this possible location and began their search.

"I've found a gold nugget!" Nicole cried out, "and another and another!" She put these into a small cloth pouch and soon added a few nuggets Gabriel and Jean-Pierre were able to find. Nicole said, "I'll take these gold specimens to Paris for an assay of their value." After she had carefully secured the pouch inside her backpack, she sat down beside Gabriel while Jean-Pierre finished a detailed drawing of the location of this valuable vein.

Before returning to the river, the three expedition

members stood quietly together for a few moments in thankfulness. Their discovery of the gold vein was like having a secret bank account in Nature, and they were certain now that expenses would be met to finance the search, development and distribution of the gray pebbles.

They made their way down the steep slopes of the cliffs and cautiously crossed the swift-flowing river again with steady footing that allowed them a safe journey. It was time then for a picnic celebration at the water's edge in full view of the miraculous cliffs! The hungry adventurers sat down on comfortable ground and enjoyed a satisfying meal in silent companionship, while cherishing the wonder of this amazing day before returning to the FRIENDSHIP.

# The Recurring Dream

*T*hat night, as Gabriel drifted into a gentle sleep amid visions of gold nugget mountains, his angel of the pebbles appeared again in his dream to say, "There is even more to share with you about the small gray pebbles. All things have consciousness, and the movement we did with our hands and fingers created a force field of energy that brought a particular response from the pebbles."

"The patterning," the angel continued, "activates the memory within the pebbles of their tremendous capacity for power. This power translates into what you recognize as heat and purification, Gabriel. The pebbles are to be activated to the full use of the power that was created within them. This is their purpose now, and this is their gift."

"To obtain heat from their power, for example, the pattern is rather like the 'on' control for the energy current of your electric stove. By reversing the pattern, the pebbles will return to a resting state. Your engineers will know how to duplicate the energy patterns you and

I created with our hand and finger movements, and the pebbles will respond in the same way as they did for us," the angel disclosed.

"And," she resumed, "one vital element to the process is that the people be reminded to express thankfulness to the pebbles for the power they are offering. This gratitude from the users completes the cycle of giving and receiving. Thankfulness in receiving finalizes the process beyond the mechanics involved," she stressed.

"Gabriel, you will remember to tell Nicole and Jean-Pierre all that I have given you this night. We are in their dreams as well, but as yet they do not remember anything by morning. What you tell them, however, will seem familiar. We are relying on you to carry our message."

"Yes, I promise to tell them everything."

"We greatly thank you, Gabriel." And, with a smile of affection, the angel departed.

# Commencing the Mission

$\mathcal{F}$ollowing the discovery of the gold vein, Nicole traveled by train into Paris to have the nuggets analyzed for their purity and weighed at the assayer's office. For the security of so important a mission, Nicole did not make known the location of the gold find, but instead told the official that the nuggets were a gift. The implication was true, for the vein of gold was indeed Nature's gift to the three pioneers of a new energy source for the world. Nicole intuitively knew that it was essential to hold all information in secret about the gold vein and the gray pebbles until this energy source was available to many, many people in the world.

The gold assayed at a high value, and Nicole exchanged it for a large sum of money in French francs before she left the city. Using some of these funds, the Honorés rented a plane for the weekend and began in earnest their search for the soft, gray pebbles. Nicole had circled the foothill region on a map of the Pyrenees mountains which border France and Spain. This area seemed the only possible one in or near France for the proper geological forces that could have shaped the pebble of

Gabriel's dreams.

During the search, Jean-Pierre neatly landed their small airplane on several rustic runways that were scattered throughout the countryside. At each stop, the three Honorés walked into the nearby foothills searching the ground for any indication of the pebbles. Without having found a clue, it was quite late when they returned home to the boat that first evening. There was little conversation at the supper table in the galley. The probability of ever finding the small gray pebbles in so vast a world seemed to overwhelm the seekers. However, as they prepared for bed, each offered the other some words of encouragement for the proposed hunt the next day.

Fortunately, the angel of the pebbles appeared in Gabriel's dream during that night. She pointed to a small cave beneath an outcropping of rock in the foothills of the Pyrenees mountains near where the three seekers had been the previous day. With great love flowing from her heart, she smiled upon Gabriel and said, "A splendid surprise is awaiting you three explorers in your forthcoming search." Gabriel happily shared this angelic disclosure at breakfast, for it was one dream he surely could not forget.

Hopes were high as the undaunted explorers departed for the airport. They flew to the south again and landed on an airstrip at the base of the familiar foothills. The Pyrenees mountains towered majestically above the Honorés as they walked in search of the pebbles. In case they unknowingly strayed onto private lands and were questioned, Nicole carried a paper with her which stated she was a certified geologist. This credential might be necessary to present to an inquirer. They could not, of course, admit the true nature of their search.

As Gabriel scanned the hillsides, his keen vision detected a significant rock outcropping in the distance. His feet moved swiftly in response to his desire to run toward that site. He was at the outcropping in what seemed an instant, and there he discovered a small cave almost hidden from view. He entered it cautiously, and shortly after his eyes became accustomed to the semi-darkness, he spied a soft, gray pebble on the floor of the cave that matched exactly the one of his dreams. Gabriel sat down at the cave entrance and placed the pebble on the ground before him. With a movement of his hands and fingers over the pebble in the patterning he had been taught, there instantly appeared seven more pebbles!

Gabriel shouted in jubilation, "Jean-Pierre! Nicole!

Come quickly! Look what I have found! See what's happened!" Nicole and Jean-Pierre were not far from the entrance to the cave when they heard Gabriel's call, and they responded immediately. All three stepped inside and discovered many, many more pebbles embedded in the earthen walls and the floor of the cave. The excitement of the moment was so intense that it sent all three explorers out on the hillside to laugh and shout and hug each other in sheer joy.

When their exuberance had subsided, Jean-Pierre mentioned, "The pebbles will need to be put to test later for their heating and purifying capabilities. For now, however, I feel confident these are the true pebbles of our search." He then recorded in his workbook the exact location of the cave and made another map of the general area, while Gabriel and Nicole gathered a few more pebbles to take back.

The three left the cave and strode down to a village they'd seen just over a hill from where their plane was parked. Jean-Pierre went into the local tavern and inquired about the ownership of the general area recorded on his map. He explained that he and his wife were geologists and had an interest in unusual rock outcroppings such as they had just observed. At first, some of the villagers thought that the hillside area belonged to the government, but then they noted on Jean-Pierre's drawing that the place in question was just below the public lands. They all seemed to chatter at once in their eagerness to tell Jean-Pierre it belonged to an elderly shepherd and his wife who grazed sheep there.

"You can find the couple at the very east end of this street in the white cottage with a blue door framed in climbing red roses," explained the tavern owner. Jean-Pierre thanked these people for their helpfulness and then joined the waiting Nicole and Gabriel.

Together they walked in the direction given. As they approached the white cottage, its blue door was thrown open and a gentle little country lady stood smiling upon them through eyes as blue as her front door. She invited them in and said immediately, "My husband and I know why you three have come here today. An angel appeared in my dreams last night and told me about the cave on our property, about its contents, and about the three pioneers of a new energy who would be coming to our village." The elderly shepherd added that both he and his wife understood well the necessity for secrecy.

Now all this information was startling to the Honorés, and yet they realized how easily a major piece of their pebble puzzle had fit into place. They confided the complete details of their energy mission to this now trusted couple and asked them to be guardians of the cave.

Gabriel reached in his pocket and brought out the eight pebbles from his first test to show this couple. The shepherds couldn't determine which one he had picked up initially from the floor of the cave to create seven more. Gabriel reasoned aloud, "I think whatever pebble I multiply will remain true to itself in size, shape and color. And regardless of slight variations in the other pebbles I found today in the cave, I believe they will all have the same qualities for heating and purifying."

He then took a pebble from Nicole's sample bag and performed the patterning over it. The kindly couple smiled in awe as they looked upon eight pebbles which had suddenly appeared where only one had been. Gabriel placed this second batch of pebbles with the others in the sample bag, and all would be tested for their capabilities as soon as the Honorés returned to the FRIENDSHIP.

After some discussion on how best to proceed in protecting the contents of the cave, a plan was developed and agreed upon. The Honorés gave these trusted shepherds a good sum of French francs with which to build a little mountain house for themselves on their land beside the cave. The couple happily agreed to such a course of action. This would allow them to offer the cottage in the village to their son and family who lived in Paris, but longed to return to their beloved southern homeland by the Pyrenees.

The strategy was for the shepherds to use the cave as a root cellar to hold vegetables from their small garden. The entrance would be closed by a wooden door with a crossbar typical of the area, so that the cave would appear to be just a simple place for food storage. The gentle guardians of the pebbles assured the Honorés that they understood the importance of what they had agreed to do. "We will not reveal anything about this assignment to anyone, not to close friends or family, not even to our dear son. We know it is much too early in this project for any others to be aware of the pebbles."

"It's similar," the shepherd continued, "to the gestation period for a lamb which remains protected and hidden within the mother ewe until it is strong enough to be in the world. I am certain there will be no suspicion in the village over our choice of a homesite because we have spoken openly of a desire to have our son and family return to the home village. And furthermore, a recent and very successful sale of breeder rams brought us extra funds which the villagers might logically expect us to use in the building of a new home."

As to the connection with the Honorés, the shepherds agreed to say only that they had made friends with these people who liked to explore the geology of the area and would probably come again from time to time. The Honorés and the guardians shook hands on all their agreements and bade each other farewell for now.

The return flight was filled with lively conversation in the cockpit. What an exciting turn of events since they had left the FRIENDSHIP that morning! Nicole discussed the necessity of refraining from any talk concerning the pebbles whenever they were in public. In this respect, Jean-Pierre strongly cautioned them by saying, "There are some people on the planet who would delight in grabbing all these wonderful pebbles for themselves and then demand great sums of money for just one small stone."

"I really believe all people on earth sometime in the future will be responsible and caring, and then there will be no need to protect anyone or anything from greed or harmful use of power," Gabriel speculated, "but for now I'll be careful."

Then, all three Honorés consented to take extreme precautions in preventing disclosure of their mission's high purpose. Before long, the hungry explorers were once again seated at the little table in the galley, feasting on Nicole's nurturing supper. Afterwards, the clean-up chore was speedily accomplished, for they were eager to test the pebbles. And, yes, all the soft, gray pebbles were true to their nature. Each proved its capacity for both heat and purification.

 # The Mission Expands

N ow it was time to explore the far-away areas on Nicole's world map of geological possibilities. More gold was secured from the cliff site and exchanged for money to finance the journeys. Jean-Pierre took a leave-of-absence from his work and Nicole accepted no new consulting jobs, so they would be free to travel. Gabriel's schoolbooks, however, were always included in the minimum luggage they would carry aboard the large commercial jet airplanes, the smaller propeller ones and the various vehicles used in their search for pebbles at other locations.

In the north of Norway where the Sami live in that part of Lapland, the Honorés made a second find. Near the Swedish border, they discovered a partly hidden cave in a shallow outcropping of rock with all major aspects similar to the site near the Pyrenees. Gabriel crawled on hands and knees inside the narrow entrance to find many partly exposed gray pebbles. He collected several samples and returned for Nicole and Jean-Pierre to examine them. Then he placed these stones on the soft tundra and performed his multiplying patterns, with the immediate reward of many more pebbles. "It's the miracle all over again!" he announced triumphantly.

As it was in France, the Honorés quite astonishingly met up with the would-be-guardians. A young Sami couple approached from the midst of their reindeer herd. The man, speaking some English, said, "We expected you three explorers ever since my recent daydream about pebbles as I dozed on the tundra beside my herd."

"Because we are nomads in this wild land, we will be making infrequent inspection of the cave. But do not be concerned. My wife and I have grazing rights for our herd through a passage way where this very cave is located. All the pebbles will be safe in our uninhabited area," he promised.

Jean-Pierre made very meticulous notes and sketches of the cave site, because the endless expanse of unchanging tundra made it difficult to find reliable points of reference for one unfamiliar with the landscape. The Sami herder wrote his name and place of contact for the Honorés, who did the same for him so they would know how to reach each other before the Honorés returned in the future. Gabriel and then Nicole and Jean-Pierre shook hands with the Sami couple to bind their contract. Next, Jean-Pierre presented a large payment in

Norwegian kroner to compensate for their guardianship.

Numerous possible sites in other parts of the world proved unproductive, but the earlier finding of two pebble locations buoyed up the explorers in their global search. At last, in the bush country of Australia, a sighting of familiar rock outcropping sent the seekers scrambling up a brush-covered hillside to reach it. The sun beat down with unusual intensity, and the Honorés were forced to slow their steps in spite of their eagerness. Finally, they came to the outcropping and found relief from the heat in its cool cave. There, embedded in the dirt were the familiar pebbles.

As it happened at the other two sightings, all the necessary pieces came together. An aborigine appeared from seemingly nowhere and walked directly toward them with light and easy steps. His bare feet were quite accustomed to the scorching heat of the earth, and his body looked as if it took no notice of the blistering sun. In a place of peace within himself, the Australian bushman approached Jean-Pierre and said, "I know exactly the role I am to take in this event."

He helped Jean-Pierre make a map of the area, and then both men exchanged names and addresses for future contact. Jean-Pierre extended a generous amount of

Australian dollars to this native guardian of the pebble cave, and the contract was sealed with vigorous handshakes.

The Honorés returned to France carrying many pebbles from the two new sites, after having tucked them into every conceivable corner of their limited luggage. Seated together once more in the living quarters of the FRIENDSHIP, they each leaned back into the comfort and pleasantness of home to savor the joy of the exploration and the joy of the return.

"Who could possibly have designed such a marvelous adventure without it seeming to be pure fairy tale!" said Gabriel. "I've even managed to successfully complete my school lessons in spite of the unusual conditions of my traveling classroom."

"You've returned to France with such an expanded vision of yourself," Nicole added, "and of your world, the people within it, the geography and geology, the plant and animal life. No schoolbook could ever be expected to duplicate such an experience."

Gabriel marveled aloud over the amazing happenings in his life in the short time he'd become a beloved part of the Honoré family. And Nicole and Jean-Pierre agreed, saying their own lives had taken a surprising direction since Gabriel's coming. And they were filled with gratitude for all that had occurred.

The jubilant but weary travelers of the world soon retired to their beds and were soothed into sleep by the familiar rocking of the FRIENDSHIP in the river Seine.

# Trusted Friends are Enlisted

Following their high spirited return to the FRIENDSHIP, Nicole and Jean-Pierre considered how best to proceed with the next step. They had been good friends for years with two very skilled design engineers they'd met in France, when all four of them were new graduates on first jobs. Nicole and Jean-Pierre simultaneously concluded that these two capable and reliable men should be contacted at once and presented with an invitation to design proper devices for the small but miraculous pebbles.

The outcome of the Honorés' presentation to these engineers was an immediate and eager response to accept this challenging opportunity. The engineers asked that two others be solicited as members of the group. Before long, this skilled team of three men and a woman were enthusiastically engaged in their work. Concepts and designs flowed without hesitation from their minds, filling page after page of drafting paper. Events moved much faster than the Honorés or the engineers could have imagined. The pebble project seemed to gather momentum with astounding speed.

Gabriel's pebble dreams continued, and from them he could give added essential information to the engineers whenever they reached an impasse.

Within a few months, several devices were constructed and tested by the project participants. Soon it became evident to those involved that one excellent design had been developed to provide heat in the preparation of food. Another of their designs proved superior for the warming of dwellings. And of the devices they had constructed for water purification, their simplest design performed best in all tests.

With money from the gold vein, the Honorés set up a small factory and began production. The entire project, however, continued in secrecy. Because the pebbles were to be inserted after the devices were made, the factory employees were completely unaware of the magnitude of these simple inventions they were assembling.

While the devices were being produced and stored in a large warehouse, Gabriel was occupied with the multiplication of the pebbles. These he boxed and stacked beside the devices. When the warehouse became filled, production was temporarily halted until the next plan could be implemented.

# Global Contact

*I*t was now time to take the major step of talking with the Heads of State of the poorer nations around the world. They were individually contacted in person by Jean-Pierre and Nicole, along with Gabriel. The three simple inventions were demonstrated over and over again and were received everywhere with enormous enthusiasm. Heads of these governments expressed the wish that their people live more comfortably with sufficient, inexpensive heating for their shelters and their cooking, and with a simple means of purifying their domestic water supply.

In every struggling nation, secret stockpiling of the new devices began, and in France, production of both components resumed. With monies from the gold vein, the Honorés helped pay for subsequent demonstration and distribution of the three inventions whenever a nation had too limited a treasury to accomplish this task on its own.

With amazing swiftness, the heating and purifying devices were soon in many homes and huts and makeshift shelters of the people of these disadvantaged countries. The joy of this astonishing happening was felt throughout each of the lands affected. It was not long before people of the more affluent countries of the world took notice of startling changes within the poorer nations, and there was a call from them to be provided with the same opportunity.

At first, the Heads of affluent countries were reluctant to encourage any use of the new devices because so much industry and commerce were based upon existing modes of energy. However, it soon became clear to these leaders that they could not forbid this new energy source within their country's borders. And gradually all nations adjusted to the change.

The global use of clean, inexpensive pebble energy to heat and purify brought an outpouring of thankfulness from its billions of inhabitants. And this gratitude flowed over the planet in a wonderful expression of unity never before experienced!

# Fulfillment
## of a Dream

*T*he creative minds of thousands and thousands of people were busily engaged in developing new uses for the remarkable pebbles. Some people were considering advanced devices to purify the multitude of streams and rivers, ponds and lakes. Even the great oceans and polar caps were taken into account. Others were contemplating intricate devices for operating various means of transportation. A great surge of ideas enveloped the world kindled by the gladness and optimism over the unlimited possibilities of the little gray pebbles.

Gabriel had brought about such an increase of these pebbles that enough would be available for some years to come. His dream angel then told him, "You need not be concerned with the supply aspect any more, Gabriel. There will be people knowing how to multiply the pebbles as the need arises, and there will be those finding more uses for them in the future."

One night, the angel of the gold and the angel of the pebble appeared together before the young and faithful

Gabriel in a most vivid dream to say, "Thank you, for a job well done! You and Nicole and Jean-Pierre so diligently listened to us, and together we have brought forth new and better ways for the people to be on earth. Now it is time for the three of you to go play in this new world you helped to create. Enjoy in Joy! And do so with our fullest Love."

The Honorés had successfully completed their part in the grand Pebble Mission. Now it was time to visit again the trusted guardians and thank these keepers of the pebbles for their very important part of the Mission. For awhile the three sites were to remain secret. But before long, the public would be invited to visit the pebble caves and ponder the humble beginnings for such remarkable energy.

Following their heartwarming contact with each of these guardians, the Honorés traveled for some months around the world, enthralled by its beauty and by the wondrous new changes occurring. They would, of course, always be available for consultation and advice wherever it was needed. But for now, they were simply enthusiastic users and admirers of the new energy source. Who would have suspected that one small gray pebble appearing in a boy's dream would have played such a powerful role for good on the planet!

# THE END

• • • but not the end

 *Addendum*

Some time later, Gabriel met with Mademoiselle Martinez at l'orphelinat du Paris. She told Gabriel she'd read about the Honoré family in a French news magazine and was thrilled to learn about the magnificent gift they'd made available to the world. Mademoiselle confided that she now realized how important it was for Gabriel to have been exactly his unusual, though exasperating, self while he'd lived at the orphanage.

"Furthermore," she confessed, "long, long ago I myself could see fairies and elves in our family garden, and even talk with the birds and trees. You have inspired a remembrance within me that I shall cultivate. I'll not hide that part of myself any longer. I understand full well what the outcome has been to the world because of your 'nonsense' that I was so upset with. Please forgive me for being so blind to your beautiful uniqueness!"

Gabriel reached out to shake her hand in acknowledgment of his forgiveness, but instead threw his arms about Mademoiselle in a warm embrace.

All the frustrations and misunderstandings that had ever occurred between these two were instantly and forever dissolved. Only a deep bond of friendship prevailed from that day forward.

There are only two ways
to live your life.
One is as though nothing
is a Miracle.

The other is as if
everything is.


- Albert Einstein

# Pronunciation Guide

Gabriel ... Gab-ray-el

Mademoiselle Martinez ...Mad-mwha-zell Mar-teen-ay

naiveté ...nie-eve-i-tay

le parc d'attractions ... leh park da-trak-sea-ohn

Nicole ... Nee-coal

Jean-Pierre Honoré ... Zjohn-Pee-air On-nar-ray

au revoir ... oh re-vwha

l'orphelinat du Paris ... lor-fell-ee-nah due Pare-ree

Renault ...Rheh-no

Seine ... Senn  (river in France)

baguette ...bag-get

croissant ...kwa-sohn

Capitaine ...Cap-ee-ten

Pyrenees ... Peer-ree-nay  (mountain range)

franc ...frahnc  (French money)

Sami ...Saa-mee

kroner ...crow-ner  (Norwegian money)

aborigine ...a-ba-rij-i-nee  (native inhabitant)

# About the Author

As a child in Southern California, author Carol Hovin roamed happily among roses and poinsettias, pepper and avocado and lemon trees, and the many more delights in the family garden. After a ten-year career in Fashion Merchandising, she and her agriculture scientist husband created gardens wherever they lived as they raised their own children.

Today, in retirement on a small farm in the Northern Rockies, their love of Nature continues undiminished. Deer in the hayfield and occasional visits from coyote, fox, porcupine, pheasant and sandcrane add another fascinating dimension to the farmstead. During the snows of winter, Carol does the major portion of her writing.

The author compiled and edited an earlier publication, TWELVE HERBS OF LIGHT, Clarestar, 1986, which is now out of print.

# Synopsis

Fifteen brief chapters and approximately 12,000 words. This manuscript offers the essence of imagination and hope to young readers for happier ways in which all people might experience our planet.

Gabriel's early years in a French orphanage contradict the subsequent glorious outcome. He struggles in his interactions with adults because of his exceptional ways of knowing what others do not. At the age of nine, Gabriel is at last adopted by a warm, loving couple, Nicole and Jean-Pierre Honoré and shares their boat home on the river Seine.

The Honorés, professionally trained geologists, assist Gabriel in the interpretation of his precocious pebble dreams. In a series of adventures, pebbles corresponding to those of Gabriel's dreams are found in uncommon locations in the world. This discovery eventually leads to unique ways to heat food and dwellings and to purify water. The inhabitants of the planet are magnificently benefitted because of the trust by a few given a young boy and his revelations.